Love me now and always

Stunningly vulnerable in appearance(Love doesn't have secrets)

By

Hilda Paul

Table of Contents

<u>Chapter One</u>

dark and brooding piano music) (upbeat R&B music) - Would you mind, Leanna? Are you all right?
Sorry about that. I'm in good health. Oh my gosh, I think I'm talking way too much. You're free to do as you choose. - I'm going to share something with you that you might find interesting. - [Man] Alright. - I'm not sure how you'll handle it. Aim. - [Man] Fire!

- My hair is thinning because of alopecia areata. - What is Alopecia? Yes, I'm thinking of hair loss alopecia. - [Leanna] You're absolutely right. - Oh, oh. "I knew you'd have an issue with this," I said to Leanna. Leanna, don't worry about it, I'm fine. My cousin owns it, in fact. It's a great idea. So, do you have a full head of hair or not? - I'd be happy to demonstrate for you.

It doesn't need to be that that. Please tell me you're okay. Yes, yeah. - [Man] I'm cool. That's awesome. - [Leanna] Is that what you mean?

You appear exhausted. - Yeah, I'm fine, I'm fine. In fact, I urgently require the use of the restroom, so would you mind waiting for me over there? I'll be back in a minute. You know about food? Brandon?

Bye. In the mood for a little R&B? - [Radio DJname]'s is Right now it's 12 p.m. on the coast of North Carolina. Mrs. Smith's Salon, located on Shipyard Boulevard, deserves a big shout-out. - Girl. Nelly is the new girl I hired to help out around here. Her hair really does look awful on her. How are you going to work in a hair salon if your hair is worse than the customers? In other words, - (laughs) Miss Smith, you need to put a stop to this. - After all, it's true that she asked me.

If she could earn her paycheck early, would she be able to bail her boyfriend out of prison? It's like, what the hell is going on here? - Do not say such things about my private life, please. - Not at all and even if I wanted to, you don't provide me enough of a platform from which to work. What do I have? In the past few years, I've had the pleasure of meeting you and your mother. When you initially learned about alopecia, neither of you told me. - Some aspects of my life I'd prefer not to discuss.

I understand and appreciate that. But every now and then, you've gotta let it all out, girl. You must remove it from your breasts. The two of them. - Is there anything I can do? Sophia: - There you go. "Well, when I was around nine years old...?" Leanna sighs. Hurry up, your bus is about to arrive. Did your mother say anything to you when you got home? (suspenseful atmospheric music) In reality, she didn't need to.

After a few days, we found ourselves in my room, and... Why don't you tell me who you are, Leanna?
"Leanna?" (muffled sobs) Leanna? What's going on with you, Leanna? Melancholic string music fills the air as [Leanna] sobs. In other words, that's the beginning of the whole thing. Then there were the classmates, the people down the street, the gossip, and the personal connections. It's understandable that Mrs. Smith is sad for you, but it's time to put it behind you. That is not a concern of yours.

That lovely man God has in store for you is all you need to worry about. - Yes, with the grace of God. In terms of a man, I'm not ready yet. - Although I know what you are going through, don't give up on God's plan for your life. You act like though you've lost an arm or something. It's time to move on. - That's exactly it. "Get over it," is a common refrain. But it's not as simple as it sounds!. Your hair is a constant reminder of how stunning you are everywhere you go.

What about those of us who don't possess it? Alopecia will be the least of your concerns should you ever use that tone with me again. - [Leanna] I'm sorry for the inconvenience. - Right now. - Music: Uplifting R&B - What's going on with him right now? Could you please make some progress? Is it possible he slipped and fell off the trolley? - Hi, there. Then, what's yours?

I'm sorry, but I have a really important meeting to attend. Please, tell me your name so I can identify you. I have to know. - My apologies for the inconvenience. - All I care about is finding out your identity. - What's the deal? Due to the fact that I would be a fool to not. Leanna laughs and says, "Um, I'm sorry. We don't have to stay here. (sad orchestral music) We can handle it on our own.

The fact that I have nowhere else to go isn't a big deal. Moreover, Robin is on her way. - What's your name, Robin? What did you do to get her to come here? What's next? (laughs) - That's fine. Just keep an eye out for Sophia's son. I think he's supposed to be delivering dessert. - All right, thanks for your time. - I'm unable to do this task. - [Leanna's] response: It's Robin, Robin! There's something wrong about her.

How do I know what this is? - [Robin] I'm not sure what you were referring to when you described this event to me. - Would you have come if I told you? What's going on? - That's not right! Yes, I'm sorry. When you say you're a Christian, what do you mean? - All I need is a little help from you.
What can I do for you? It's time for diaper changes? - Not a thing. - So, exactly, what do you think? Adieu, I'm going to the actual thing.

There's just enough for Robin. I'm sorry to hear that. There he is. I ran into him at the hairdresser earlier today. What? You let him go? Do you not understand what's going on with you? - Simply a matter of bad luck. In fact, I was on the verge of hitting him with my automobile. This isn't anything I set out to do. The man in front of me has blocked my path out. - This is for you, ladies, from Sophia, my aunt.

Let me know if you have any questions. Hi. - Hello there, my name is.
It's going to be a terrific time. My life was in danger today because I couldn't remember your name, you know. My apologies for being so late. Why are you rushing now? The youngsters, at least. - Leanna, you should know that I think you're gorgeous. Please come back again. - Oh, thank you! - What are you talking about?
Let me know if you need anything. - Who or what are you avoiding at any costs? A relationship, marriage, and children aren't in my immediate future.

What have you done? I understand why you're on the run. The man asks, "Are you fine?" - Sorry, I hadn't planned on it happening like that.

Chapter Two

- I had a brilliant idea with Terrence. Just since you asked, I'll stay here while you two head over to Jamaican Comfort Zone next door to help out with the party. Robin: - Oh, my goodness... No, he's not taking you to his house. It's not like that. - Let's do this.
Okay, that's OK. - Goodbye, kids, and have a good time!

Miss Smith is your aunt, although I didn't know it. - You're right, she is amazing. I'm in love with your hair, too. Oh, thank you. Do you have any idea what she does on a daily basis? - I'm not sure if I did, but I'm not sure either. Am I

overlooking something with her behavior?
There's nothing wrong with that, I was simply
curious. What drew you to Wilmington, and
why? - As far as I'm concerned, I'd say... My
father served in the military.

When he was on vacation in Portland, England,
he ran into my mother.
- That's great. - And, uh, he died when I was
around six years old, which was a real bummer.
To cut a long story short, I chose to attend this
university. So how did you end up here? - It's a
long tale. In high school, I had a lot of
difficulties. And I barely made it to college. My
professor was fantastic; he was a really cool
guy. I finally made it there.

For as long as he supported my dreams, I
always believed he was right. In my mind, this
code would allow me to win the lottery every
time. Consequently, I dropped out of college at
the end of my junior year. - Okay, I'm not sure
what you're saying. When you were so near to
the end, why did you quit out? - Regardless of
whether it was pure chance or the code
working, I'd say I've hit the lottery for... I won
1.5 million dollars in the lottery.

Wow. My only source of provision is the Lord,
so it's a good thing I don't believe in winning
the lotto. - [Waitress] How are all of you doing?
- Yeah, I'm good, thank you. Is there anything
else that I could possibly acquire for you? We
don't need anything, everything's fine, thanks.
I believe that everything is going to be all right.
- [Waiter] Excellent. - Hey, you want to go
dance? - What time is it?
- Yeah. - Sure.
- Let's go. (calm jazz music)

- What? - You're gorgeous. You are in point of
fact. - On this Monday morning, I hope that
everyone got a good night's sleep. A new
member of staff has joined us. I would like to
take this opportunity to welcome Tasha
Sprinkle. Tasha, this is our senior leadership
team.
- Hello. - This is Sergio speaking to you, Tasha.
Nick. Carla. Robin. As well as Leanna.

- Hi. - I'd want to take this opportunity to extend
a warm welcome to Tasha as she joins our team.
She brings a great deal of value to the table. -
Yes.

Are you there, Robin? - To satisfy my natural inquisitiveness, I was wondering how exactly we may make Tasha a useful part of what we already have in place. - She possesses... oh, I see what you mean. - [Leader] Oh, okay. Now, I'm going to bring another level with me, and with that level, I'm going to bring you up to the standard, and I'm going to guide you to victory. - You got it, the win. We have more excellent news to share with you.

The individual who will serve as the leader of our next project has been selected. Leanna. You will serve as the leader of our subsequent project. Could Leanna come with us up here? (applause) Congratulations, Leanna.
- It's my pleasure. - [Leader] Greetings, Tasha. We have a significant amount of work to complete. Could you just get to work? - It looks like we're good to go, so let's get started. You ready to stop standing about and take a seat? It seems like we should get started. - [Tasha] Excuse me, but would you mind if I asked you a quick question?

Yes, without a doubt, how can I be of use to you? Obviously, you need to sit down. I was

under the impression that I was going to be the project manager. - [Leader] What would cause you to have such thought? - You did say that you appreciated the manner that I managed the other projects at Camille's, right?
- Yes, I did. Nevertheless, this did not imply that you would be led. So, what exactly does that signify? - That indicates that you have the potential to work your way up to lead, much like Leanna did. - Okay. I guess I understand.

Chapter Three

I see, that's wonderful, I'm relieved that you get it. I hope your day is wonderful. - She could have at least ensured that I receive a workstation or something like that. - Hello, this is Leanna Hillman checking in with you. - [The receptionist] Yes, ma'am, might you please have a seat? Okay, and I appreciate your help. Love your dress.
I am grateful to you. Hello, my name is Jessica Smith, and I'm here to sign in. - [The receptionist] Yes, ma'am, might you please have a seat? - I am grateful. What are you doing in this place, man?
- Hey! Oh, you know which part I enjoy the most, going to the doctor.

Girl, I have to ask you, do you not despise it? But here's what I think: who exactly is the new girl they hired up there in that hideous dress? - I didn't even notice. Girl, I saw you walking in with that dress. I was coming from the parking lot. It was horrible, but whatever you did to your hair looks really good. (Laughs) You had mentioned that you were planning to cut it and other things. - I am very grateful.

- I love it. - Speculate on who was the one who noticed it this time. - Is that you, Anthony?

- Oh yes, he did. Girl, I'm sorry, but I don't like him anyway. Bye. Guys typically aren't very good at paying attention to things that are significant to

They don't give a second thought to our hair like we do. It was a big hit with him, so I'm going to maintain it that way.

- It's best to keep it that way, as well. Don't be concerned about him; it's only your hair. However, I'd want to ask you a question: Are you off today? - Oh, yes, mm-hm.

This is a major favor for me. It's a mystery.

- I require a full hair makeover. However, I require assistance with the finishing of the edges. "[Receptionist]" asks. Who is Miss Hillman, by the way? Pleased to meet you Leanna. What's up? - I'm fine, thanks for asking. By the way, the decor in here is quite nice.

Like, the lobby and everything, it's very
stunning. You know, your mother was the
driving force behind that. - Thank you! She
expressed an interest in my taste when you
brought her along to your appointment the last
time, so I was motivated to redecorate. I'm glad
you like it. - That's Mom, I believe.
- Hm. You were just telling me about a date the
last time you were here, weren't you? Let's have
a look at the results. - Oh, no. I'd rather not
discuss it.

"Wow," you're saying. It's... a... It was
enjoyable, however I erred by going on a
second date. I'm sorry, I was a little
overconfident and told him. Fortunately, he
talked too much, so it's not a problem. It's better
that you're aware now, don't you think? Trust
me, when the proper person comes along, you'll
know it because he won't care about your
feelings, okay? Let's get started, shall we?

I'm going to close the door and ask you to
remove your wig for me. - Fair enough.
- Alright, I'll go with that. So, how are you
doing today? - [Leanna] It hurts a little. - It's a
little sensitive.

- You're right. There you go: - Is that all right?
So what you should do is take the pain medicine
I gave you the last time so that you can take that
for whatever type of headaches you get. It's
supposed to be gone by now, right?

Also, I'd like you to return in approximately six
weeks to check how things are doing, because
these injections aren't always successful. The
truth is, there is no treatment for hair loss, but
this may encourage hair growth, and everyone's
experience is unique, so come back in six weeks
and we'll see if we can get some peach fuzz??
Moreover, we'll go cautiously at first. You're
going through so much right now, Leanna, but
the stress isn't going to help. Please take care of
yourself.

It will take some time for your body to heal
before your hair grows back, so be patient and
don't worry too much about it. I'm sure
everything will work out, right? Alright, so
please pray for me tonight when you go to
church. There you go! (laughs) You forgot.
Alright, that's fine.
Please excuse my tardiness; I must leave now.
piano music with a tinge of sadness In response

to your appeal some time ago—and my affirmative response—Lord, Despite the difficulties, I still say yes. On occasion, I prefer to be by myself.

In that case, the answer is a resounding yes, at least for the time being. That's what my spirit tells me, baby: God is good. He is, in fact. He is, in fact. He's a master, a master. - Do you have self-control? - Honey, you can't control yourself when you're possessed by the spirit. - Hallelujah! Yes, my Lord and Savior.

That's right. - Why did it take you so long to get back to me? Why did it take you so long?
(Leanna gasps)
I was occupied. - [Robin] Let's swap places, shall we? - What's the deal? Hi.
- Hello. - My stomach's churning because of Mrs. Siggly. What was the hold-up?
I was occupied. - That's OK. Because you're so mysterious at times, I had to inquire. - Let yourself have a good time at the conference.
- That's OK.

But in the Lord neither man nor woman is whole without each other. Amen. Because just as the woman is a product of the male, so too is the man a product of the woman, but everything is of God. Amen. Is it appropriate for a woman to pray uncovered to God? If even nature cannot teach you that a man's long hair is a source of embarrassment, then what can we expect from society? But if a woman has long hair, please listen to me.

The fact that her hair is provided to her as a covering is an honor, amen. Y'all women, you're so far out in the world that you don't even know what's best for you. However, when I got the news about you, Leanna, my heart ached. Because, honey, God put it on my heart to inform you that the word has been given to you, sweetheart. It's something to ponder. Revealed: The word is here. Alright?

In order to let him know you're interested - [Robin] You should have at the very least called. - Oh, I do hope he's aware of my enthusiasm. I think he's in good shape. - I'm very sure he's intrigued as well. - How did you find out? Oh, please! It's time to get started. Just for you. Hi. - What's the big deal? To let you

know that I've been thinking of you, this is just
a note.

Chapter Four

It's possible that after work, I'd have something
else planned. It would be great if you could
come back the following day. I figured we
could get along. - [Tasha Voiceover] Oh, I just
hope he didn't come to collect me for child
support, because I just started this job. Is this
even his place? - The time has come. Let's go
for it. Tasha, the narrator, says:
Who are Terrence and Leanna? First my job,
then my man....... the sound of a drowsy guitar
Terrence: Do you want to go out for a drink?

- I decline your offer. - It'll be a lot of fun. -
Proverbs 23:20 (NKJV). "Don't drink for the
sake of being drunk, and don't eat for the sake
of becoming obese." Okay, that's OK.

- Please don't take this the wrong way. - You're right. Wow, the sky is so clear right now. Even if we came out here at night, I'm sure we'd see some amazing stars. - We could tell a good story if we did that. No, I didn't know that about the stars. The answer is no.

This is the first time I've used a star map with cylindrical projection. Terrence: (laughing) What? [Terrence] In high school, I took a course in astronomy. It's all tied together. — [Terrence] Cool. In your college years, what did you do to pass the time? In fact, I was given a full ride, but I chose not to use it. - You're going to college for free? Surely you're some kind of mad scientist. What happened? Why didn't you take it? Were you alarmed in any way? - Not at all.

[Terrence] I just want to make sure that you're not imagining things. That is an opportunity that must be missed. - No. [Terrence] C'mon, you could tell me. Come on. I didn't have any worries or concerns about anything. - Leanna. I just don't get it. You've put forth so much effort. Do you have any idea how proud your dad would be of you now at this precise second?

You've got a great opportunity at a prestigious university, and you stay there for one month before you bail out? - I didn't like it!

I get it, sweetheart, the kids are being mean; I know it's hard for you. But you won't be able to keep escaping this for good forever. If it isn't alopecia, then it can be another condition. - Something else?
- Yes! I don't even feel pretty, let alone beautiful. I don't feel good about myself. I'm sorry, Mom, but this is ruining my life! I'm sorry about what happened previously. - [Terrence] - [Terrence] It's okay. Things just sort of happen, I think. - Are we okay? - Yeah. We're good to go, yeah.

We are the ones in control of our own destinies. We are the ones in control of our own psyche. (Laughter) Sergio, please bring up the video. The one you showed it to me the other day, which was about the pool and the person who was diving into it. Nick, I need you to come over here and look at those layouts right now. - Um... Could I bring my wings with me? Yes, Nick, let's go on with this. - Yeah, Nick. (he chuckles) Alright, I'll see you later. - See ya.

Did you previously pull it up to the proper
level? - [Sergio] Please give me a moment, I
need to find it.

You need to make the switch from 3G to 4G as
quickly as possible. The most sluggish mobile
device in the world.
I mean, really, come on, man. What's up with
everyone? Hey! Girl! I felt obligated to fill you
in on what had been going on. Do you
remember the other day when I was telling you
about my lover and what he's like?
No, I don't speak to you at all. - (laughs) We are
such good friends despite the fact that she is so
weird. - No.
Girl, he won't stop phoning me up. He is putting
a lot of emphasis on the marriage problem. He
is ready to make a commitment, but I am not
sure what it should be.

I mean, he is talking to some other woman, but
we have a child together, and it is obvious that I
love him, so I'm just trying to figure out what I
should do. I should do, I mean, he is talking to
some other woman. I'm not sure if I should just
take the plunge and settle down, so I'm looking
to you for some guidance. Oh, you were

inquiring about his name, weren't you? - No. - It is known by the name Terrence. You most likely do not know him, but it's possible that you do. However, his aunt is the proprietor of that salon on Castle Street. You are aware of Miss Smith.
(Leanna hacks) Do you think she's okay? Okay, from here on out, take it one bite at a time.

Chapter Five

So at this point, I'm simply trying to figure out what course of action to do. I just—All right, I've had my fill of that. - In need of a trustworthy friend.
- That's all I need to hear, honey. Okay, give me some time to mull it through, and I'll get back to you on that. - You are the best kind of buddy.
- I know. I really appreciate it, girl, because I really do need to offer him an answer of some kind, do you know what I mean? We will proceed in that manner. You should know better. Okay! Toodaloo! - Adios!

That is so strange, holy crap. [Leanna] You don't think it's a coincidence, do you? - I get the impression that the two of you aren't going to get along, honey. - Will you be coming inside? - [Leanna] (with a chuckle) Not at all. Come on, you're always making an excuse for yourself. You've never been in my pool once. Regardless, I came over here to chat to you about something, whatever it may be. - [Terrence]

Okay, talk. Maybe after we've finished eating. -
[Terrence] All right, let's go for a little swim.

We have some other clothing for you to try on,
and I think you'll really like it. - No, no, no. -
You've got to move.
What exactly are you up to right now? Oh,
come on now, don't, stop playing, stop playing,
stop playing. (dark, ominous music played by
an orchestra) [Terrence] You want to try some,
baby? [Terrence] - No. You know, I've
observed that you don't ever pray right before
you chow down on something. You certainly
never forget to pray before you eat, do you? -
No, I've never seen that. Because I want to
show respect to God and express gratitude to
him for providing me with food. I don't really
like for that though, even if it's very great.

[Leanna] And can you tell me the reason behind
that? - 'Cause I don't believe in God? Oh, are
you going to argue with me? - I don't believe in
God. Do you not agree that this is a topic that
you ought to have brought up right at the
beginning of our relationship because it was
something that was extremely significant and

important? I mean, how significant can it possibly be if it's going to take place so soon? If a lady states that she is doing something for the glory of God, then I would assume that God holds a certain amount of significance in her life. - Yeah, but I knew a large number of church females who said something along those lines.

They were helping themselves, but they'd give it up in such a careless manner. However, I don't consider myself to be a church girl because I am a Christian. - It's hard for me to know what to say to you in this situation. I'm sorry, I suppose that's what I meant. - I've got to go.
- Let's talk about it, don't. Stay here and talk to me. You are the lucky owner of such a beautiful house. - Thank you. So, according to Leanna, you're not a religious person at all. - Mommy!
- It's okay. I'm afraid that you're right, Mrs. Hillman; I don't have any faith in God. - You undoubtedly have a hunger.

You don't have any food in your place, does it seem right? - Please, please, be my mother.

It's not a big deal, sweetie; everything is going to be all right. It's simply that this pizza is delectable, it was prepared by hand, and I can definitely see where Leanna gets her cooking skills from. - Leanna is capable of doing some limited actions. After her father passed away, she was left with no other option but to pitch in and help out. Terence is the subject of this sentence. I'm aware of this, and I have no doubt that the task at hand was challenging, but, hey, she learned it from the very best. Thank you very much (insert chuckle here). Have you ever given any thought to the idea of getting married? - At each and every opportunity. I mean, how could I possibly say no to that?

Take a gander at her. - Natty To bring you food, Theese is going to require a cart that can carry a lot of weight. - [Terrence] Okay, it's just that the cuisine was incredible, and I could tell that you did an excellent job instructing Leanna. You're laying on the compliments a little too thick, aren't you? - [Leanna] Mommy. - My mother always stressed the importance of having proper manners and told me it would take you far in life. But not via the gates of heaven? - Honey, you don't have anything to worry about with

this situation. - My house, my problem. So, just
tell me, which awful being extended an
invitation for you to come here.

Chapter Six

You were kind enough to invite me to this gathering. (Referring to the Mother) You've got to be kidding me, Mr. Smarty Pants! - Just take a deep breath and relax. - Okay. There is not the slightest shred of evidence to support the existence of God! I was wondering if you could tell me where he originated from. - Just take it easy here. - You can't tell me where she came from, so, I mean, if he is real, let's say he is real, so, what differentiates him from all the other gods to make him the "one true god" that you church folks claim he is? - You can't tell me where she came from. - You can't tell me where she came from. (coughs) Let me... (coughs) May I speak to your mother?

(The mother hacks) And what exactly was the point of all of that? I'm so sorry about it. Sorry is not going to cut it in this situation. The fact that you apologized does not explain the contempt you showed toward my mother. - Simply expressing my viewpoint was all I was doing. It is not so much the content of what you said as the manner in which you said it. - Look, I was just being honest. You are familiar with the concept of telling the truth, aren't you? - Please listen carefully, because I have something important to tell you. [Terrence], what are you talking about? Come ahead, Leanna, tell me.

We're good. Just tell me, Leanna. You're absolutely right, let's just get going. - Hey, you should know that I'm exhausted, and I'm going to get going. - It is too late to drive back, so all you can do is take the couch. - Are you sure? I have no intention of damning you to damnation or doing anything else of the sort. What are you talking about, now? Oh, get over yourselves! On purpose and only for you.
- Okay. (a depressing piece played on the piano) (little drops of water are splattered) (Leanna sighs)

(door opens) (melancholic piano music) I'm so sorry about it. I'm not able to participate in this because I'm trying to be married in the near future. It was nothing more than a kiss, so

please don't feel bad about it. If that's the case,
I'm going to head on over to the television and
watch some stuff. (chuckles) (Leanna is
wearing pants) — The Father. Please accept my
gratitude for simply existing in this world as
you do. You have stated that "ask, and it shall
be given to you," and "knock, and it shall be
opened to you." Well, Lord.

I'm knocking pretty hard right now to get your
attention. I'm praying for the strength to resist
temptation while that attractive man dozes off
on that couch. Please hear my supplication. I
would want to express my gratitude to you in
advance. Amen. - How you doin' today, ma'am?
I've got a flyer for you fresh off the press, if
you're interested. You are not interested in
looking into it, are you? - Someone is following
me around and attempting to bother me, and I
don't know who it is. - Out front?
- Yeah. - Don't worry about it; I'll handle
everything myself.

Hello, Calvin! How are you doing? Listen, if
I'm going to have you sit in front of my store,
I'm going to need you to be just a little bit more
friendly, you know, friendlier with the

customers coming in and out. I'm going to need you to be just a little bit friendlier with the customers coming in and out. Please, even if it's just a tiny amount, is that okay? Okay, my pleasure, and many thanks; I truly appreciate that. - What's up, dude? Are you going to try your luck with that lottery tonight? You are a definite winner thanks to the winning ticket that I have for you. - [Terrence] No, you don't need to worry about me. - Are you sure? I don't know, man, but I get the impression that you're the kind of guy who picks three things and then five other things.

Yes, I am aware that I have your telephone number written down here; take a look. Guaranteed, you can't lose. You're going to thank me in the future, buddy. I just know it. - [Terrence] Three, one, six, zero, three, and sixteen all make up the number sixteen. No. - You girls are absolutely nuts. You get rid of your eyebrow hairs so that you can fill them in again afterwards. Stupid. (water sprays) But on the other hand, I realize that not everyone can be as flawless as I am.

I'm getting the impression that you have something against me as a person. Oh, so you've picked up on my subtle hints. Honey, if there is ever an issue between us, you can rest assured that you will be the first to hear about it. Oops! My bad. (music with a foreboding atmosphere) - [Leanna's voiceover] Lord. I require your assistance at this very moment. It is impossible for me to continue to hide. It is beyond my comprehension how something that is so straightforward may be so challenging to explain to another person.

Only three words need to be said. I have Alopecia.. It may appear to be straightforward, but there is more complexity here. I am conscious of the fact that I need to inform somebody. Someone. It's hard for me to believe that you've brought me out here in this condition. - It's just hair. - It's nothing serious. That is something that everyone seems to agree on. - I believe you're exaggerating the significance of this matter well beyond what it actually is. What will happen if Terrence appears in this location? His pitiful excuse for a behind?

- [Tasha] Simple as that: marriage. - Oh, I'm
very happy for you.
- Thank you! I had the impression that I had
already informed you that he proposed to me. I
had the impression that I had already told you.
He added that the other girl he was talking to
was trying to put pressure on him to become a
preacher or some other kind of religious leader.
She is so off her rocker. He has made it very
plain that he desires a family, and he is well
aware of the fact that I fulfill the role of a
woman far more effectively than she ever could.
(gasps) I really need to be going; I have to give
my flowers some water. (giggles) Love. - Is that
your Terrence right there?

- I truly hope not. - Hold up. What exactly is
this thing with the white girl? (knocks) Excuse
me, sir. Please come in. Could I be of use to
you in some way? Son, are you okay? -
[Terrence] I really don't know. - Are you
waiting for someone in particular? - No, sir.
Well yes, kinda. What exactly are you waiting
for then?

Oh, I'm sorry, I'm not sure. - Is there anything I
can do to assist you? It's not possible for me to

just leave you here in the parking lot to do nothing. - What exactly happens during this church service? - You are well aware of how I feel about gambling. - C'mon, it's just a $20 side bet; come on. I could hand it to you on the very first try if you wanted. - You'll need to think of something different. - Okay. Now that I think about it, another game involving a bottle, us, and each other comes to mind. - A game of spin the bottle?
(Terrence chuckles)

- Tell the truth or take the dare. I'll go ahead and start.
- Okay. Truth. - Okay, the truth, uh, well, let's see. Hmm. Who's Tasha? Mm-hm. Mm-hm?
- How the heck are you even— - Ah-ah!
- What is it that you know about her? - Provide an answer to the question. I mean, she's nothing, and that relationship was just a fling; it was a, it was a mistake.

It's over, and it's over. Period. - Okay.
It is now your turn. The question is, why haven't you gone to college? - I let something hold me back. (groovy electronic music) Tell me, what is it that you've been meaning to share with me

all this time? Something that is very difficult to express, and I believe that I will just go ahead and keep it to myself because of how difficult it is. You. Which would you rather know? To tell you the truth, I'm not sure right now. Good to know.

Have you have a boy in the house? - Yeah, certainly I do. He's seven. (upbeat piano music) [Child] Have a nice day, alligator! (the door shuts) What's going on, buddy?
How are you doing? - How you doin', man? - I'm good.
- You good? You do your homework?
- Yes. Hey, I'd like to introduce you to Leanna. Leanna, Tyrel, Tyrel, Leanna.

Tyrel, it's a pleasure to finally meet you.
- Also, it's a pleasure to meet you. Dad, do you think we could play a game?
- Sure, I guess we could play. Let me go upstairs pretty quick. I apologize for the inconvenience. - Is he a son of yours and Tasha's? - No, he is my son, and Tasha is the mother. However, he did not have a father and he desperately required one. It was just him and I. Why did you think you needed to keep this

secret from me? (Terrence takes a moment to
clear his throat.) - Just to make sure you're the

one. - [Leanna] So, tell me about some of your favorite hobbies.

Chapter Seven

Um... First things first, I'm a big fan of athletics, and second, I aspire to be an actor. So I can have a supermodel girlfriend. My dad claims you're his supermodel. (Leanna elicits a chuckle from the audience) So, you're the woman that my dad is seeing, right? - I guess. You are required to be. - [Tyrel] You are the only woman that he discusses in his conversations with other people. Oh, well that's interesting to learn. Thanks for the information. - Come on, gotta go, come on. Let go, go on.

Do you have a woman in your life who you can call a girlfriend? - Well, there's this one girl in my class who I'm nervous about approaching because I don't want to appear rude. - Why? Because I am black, she is white. - Because I am black, she is white. There are times when I wish I had a lighter skin tone. What might possibly be your motivation for wishing anything like that? Because there are just white girls in my class, I frequently have feelings of embarrassment when I speak in front of them because they do not understand what I am trying to say. - Which kind of items are we talking about? - [Tyrel] You know, things like black people on television, black people making music, etc.

You really ought to be content with your current state of being. Because of your unique worth, God purposefully fashioned you to be the way that you are. - Quite, I'm well aware of the fact that I'm unique. You're right, and you know what? I'm going to be just like you. - Like me? Why? Because you are aware that you are unique and you do not hide from the person that you are, you do not fear being yourself. (phone vibrates) Sophia is the subject of this sentence. Hello? What?

- Dr. Johnson? I do have Dr. Johnson, that's correct. I'm sorry for the inconvenience, but I can connect you to Dr. Messer on line three. I am grateful. I am here to assist you in every way possible.
- It's nice to meet you, my name is Mrs. Smith. It's been a while, but I finally got around to seeing Miss Hillman. - [Person in Charge of the

Front Desk] Oh, and may I ask what the
patient's first name is? - Hello there, my name is
Gloria. - Gloria Hillman?
- Yes. - and the nature of your relationship with
the individual being treated. - I'm her best
buddy. - I kindly ask that you take a seat while I
notify the attending physician.

The fact that you are present here. Sophia is the
subject of this sentence. Okay, thank you. - I
have a guest here for Mrs. Hillman, and I would
want to introduce them to you, Dr. Johnson. It's
my pleasure. (dreary piano music) (sighs) - May
I speak with Mrs. Smith?
- Yes. - Hi, Dr. Johnson.
- Hi. - To begin, I would want to extend my
sincerest apologies for the limited amount of
information that I am able to provide with you
owing to the fact that you are not a member of
my immediate family. You, on the other hand,
have been placed on the list of people who may
visit.

So, you're telling me that I can see her, right?
- Yes, ma'am. If it's not too much trouble, I'd
appreciate it if you'd follow me.

- Okay, good, thank you. I'm going to make you something to drink, is it all right with you? - What's up, my sweetheart? (coughs) Um, that's actually not a good moment to bring that up. This entire weekend is going to be jam-packed with activities for me. No, no, I'm not going anywhere; I'm just going to meet up with some old pals. I swear, I swear that I will let you know as soon as there is a weekend that isn't as bad as the last one, all right? Okay, bye bye. (coughs)

- Are you serious? You can't continue to be this obstinate. Oh, my heavenly God. Continue to struggle to suppress the need to open your mouth. Sophia is the subject of this sentence. It is imperative that your child be informed that her mother has recently been admitted to the hospital. I can now see where she gets all of this information on hiding things from. (insert solemn symphonic music here) I am familiar with my daughter. When I feel the moment is perfect, I will divulge the information to her. When do you think the moment will be right? When it's way past the point of no return?

You are very important to us, and we don't want to lose you. Without you, Leanna wouldn't know what to do with herself. - [Gloria] You simply do not comprehend the kind of difficulty that it has entailed for her. - Oh my gosh, all men do is talk about football all the time. He's having a good year, but you've got to give Canmuten a chance too, since he's also having a good year. I mean. - Oh, come on, Olivia, you are aware that Brady is in far better shape than you are, aren't you? - Please excuse me while I talk to my boyfriend right now, and it's great to see you again. - [Man] Thank you for taking the time to speak with me, and go Patriots! Sweetie, what are you waiting for? - [Calvin] Right before your own eyes stands the master of the lottery.

Not today, man. - Why are you so upset, seeing as how you didn't get that winning ticket? What exactly is wrong with you that you have to spend all day standing out here talking to strangers about religion? I've had enough of it. - Whoa, chill, guy. Relax, it's okay, I didn't mean anything by it, man. I'm sorry. Don't lose your cool. - All right, well, then, let me to ask you this. If God seems so real to you, then tell me where he came from. From whom did God originate? You are an expert in every field. - I didn't want to imply that I am fully knowledgeable about everything, but I will tell you, God,

He did not appear out of thin air. Right, all right. That doesn't make any sense to me at all, I'm afraid. - Hey dude, listen up, first and foremost, it's quite evident that you have a problem with God, and that's what your issue is. But think about this, think about this, and are you good with that? It is made very plain in the Bible that Christ is both the beginning and the end. Okay? The initial stage. Without him, none of this would have been possible. I mean, he's the one who invented time, air, and space, is that clear? You do realize that he is not obligated to it, right?

Due to the fact that he was the one who built it. Because we have always been present in time, air, and space, it is difficult for us to get our heads around the concept that this is happening. What do you know? You should probably focus on trying to comprehend God rather than attempting to unravel his mysteries. Do you understand why it is impossible for you to accomplish something like that? 'Cause you're not him. Look, guy. I don't know what you're going through, but I see you coming through here on a regular basis and playing these lottery tickets.

To clarify, I'm asking if it's okay if I pray for you. (they both laugh) - Right at this spot? - I don't see why not. Okay, I suppose, and certainly. - You're not embarrassed, are you? - I couldn't tell you, because I've never tried it before. I'll demonstrate everything for the very first time. Please bow your head. - [Leanna] Okay, so this is what we have based on the collection of entries that were sent in by everyone; do you have any questions? I don't think it has enough of a sexual allure.

See, now why was it that my role wasn't maintained in the campaign? It was sexually appealing. - I like it. It is suitable for all ages. - I share Sergio's opinion. If you bring back my contribution, the sex appeal, then it will be wonderful. - [Sergio] Exactly. - The company's brand, on the other hand, is not just approachable to families, but also daring. There seems to be something lacking in bold. - In my opinion, Robin's suggestion best exemplifies the brand. Their product is classified as an NGP. That's some nice girl power.

- An appeal to sex. - No. There must be something else we can think of. - Bald! I have a strong suspicion that the bald is not present. - Oh, I like it. It's daring, it's gorgeous, it exudes confidence, and it screams nice girl power. That's what it is.
Yes, I really enjoy it! - I despise it. I mean, a woman with no hair at all? That is not attractive or sexy in any way.

I mean, give this some thought. Nick, do you want an ugly woman with no hair on her head? - If I like it. She is not unattractive just due to the fact that she is bald. - That is not the way you are supposed to phrase it. On the other hand, I would anticipate such behavior from an adult child. - [Leader] Tasha, there is no need for this. Oh no, it is critical that I communicate what I mean to you. Women are expected to have long, gorgeous hair and to behave in a manner that does not result in their stealing men or their careers. - Tasha, I think we should stop here. -

Terrence does not desire a relationship with a woman who has a bald head.

Chapter Eight

Believe me, I'm aware of it. However, I really shouldn't have been... Because of this, your son is going to start referring to me as mommy. (a depressing piece played on the piano) (Tasha coughs) Robin, you need to find some security. Have I been able to get my point across? Nick, go find the security personnel! Is this, (he laughs), the reason you needed a headshot of a candidate with no hair for your campaign? Terrence is not interested in... He is unaware of the fact that you lack hair on your head.

Oh, it looks like he's about to find out now (laughs). Look at her, you baldy-locks, she's nothing more than a hepher with a bald head. Take a gander at this! - Thank you. Please don't let him know about this.

(Tasha erupts in laughter) - You baldy-locks! Take a gander at this. The woman is bald. (Chuckles) She actually has a chair! (Leanna heaves a sigh.)

(the phone vibrates) Greetings. (music on a melancholy piano) (the phone makes a clanking sound) No! No! (Leanna sobs) (sobs) No! No! (pants) Hello, Mother!

(chatter in the background is muffled) - Grace. - What? - Grace. Do you remember when I questioned your mother about the differences between Jesus and the other gods? - Yeah. Grace is the correct response, in this case. And I am aware of this now, but it is probably for the best since else I may not have recognized how much uncertainty that generated between us. - Are you perplexed? There would not have been any misunderstanding.

Oh, you don't believe that, do you? - No. A few months ago, I had every intention of picking up the phone and ending the relationship, but I chose to hold off. - [Terrence] You shouldn't be concerned about it. (Robin exhales deeply) - Wow. The beach is stunning in its beauty. What's going on? I have a feeling he's going to ask me to be his wife soon. - You are so right. Would you agree with that? - I still haven't told him.

- Wow. What is it exactly that you're looking for, Leanna? I want him to love me for the honest version of myself. But how can he when he has no idea what kind of person you really are? (Terrence chuckles) - I'm nervous, I'm not going to lie. When I had my first— oh, sorry. What are you doing at the moment?
- Just listen, just listen. When I first laid eyes on you, I immediately recognized that you were unique. Before, I was confused about what it was about you that set you apart from other people, but now I get it. I never imagined that I would get married, and I never imagined that I would fall in love.

that the Lord would create the ideal person for me to spend my life with. But I believe that he created us specifically for one another, and, uh... And you are the closest buddy I have. And the one I have devoted my life to. I just wanted to express the hope that you have the same reaction. I'd like to ask you to be my wife,

Leanna. Leanna! I am truly sorry. I have not
been truthful with you. I apologize. What
exactly are you up to? I am at long last going to
be honest with you,

And revealing the genuine me to you.
(increasingly tense and ominous tones) I'm
sorry. This is the true version of me. Just about
wherever I go—at work, at home, and in
school—I have to hide, and I'm sick of it.
Above all else, I'm sick of having to keep
secrets from you. - I believed you were aware of
this. [Leanna] What did you know, exactly? I
believed you were aware that I was aware that
you suffered from alopecia. - Who...
[Terrence]... Since the first day we met, each
time you came dangerously close to hitting me
with your car,

Aunt told me about you. I didn't care. - Know it.
Always.
- Okay, Leanna. OK. Listen. You're my angel
because I gave my life to Christ. I didn't know
grace or blessing until I met you.

Before you. I'll do whatever it takes. OK. So,
marry me? - [Leanna] No. Not you. - Listening?

Obviously. Okay. - I'm not typical. Those
who've overcome insecurities. Mine is ongoing.

If I don't love myself, how can you? Whatever
we do, this will always affect me deeply.
Regardless. Dare you? I'd be foolish not to.
Robin, guess what? What? She agreed! Robin,
come celebrate with us.

Bye. Okay, we'll inform him. Shh. [Terrence]
Hey, want to eat? Sure.
Good. Doing what? - In the car.
I have a surprise for you, Terrence. Okay.
Look! Girl. (LAUGH)

Surprise! Yes, girl.